THE FOX, THE RAVEN, & THE CASTLE CAT

WRITTEN BY JEAN PAMPLIN

ILLUSTRATED BY BEVERLY BREWER

EYE DRAW GRAPHICS

© 2020 Jean Pamplin.
All rights reserved. This information is meant to be shared but please contact
the publisher for permission to reproduce or transmit it in any form.
P. O. Box 471, Winfield, Texas 75493
Phone 903-305-8023

Published by Eye Draw Graphics
P. O. Box 471, Winfield, Texas 75493
www.eyedrawgraphics.com
Phone 903-539-6158

ISBN: 978-0-9993311-4-9

Book layout by David Lopez
Printed in the United States of America.
First Edition.

THE FOX, THE RAVEN, & THE CASTLE CAT

WRITTEN BY JEAN PAMPLIN
ILLUSTRATED BY BEVERLY BREWER

Chapter One

Raven didn't know about castles in Europe, but she did know about the Oklahoma prairie castle known as Marland Mansion. She was born on the property in a tree near the gatehouse. Raven was jet black, the kind of black that glistened silver, blue and even deep scarlet red when the sun hit her feathers just so.

A bit prideful, Raven would fly over the estate grounds, cawing at the ducks on the lakes, or in general just making noise whenever anything looked out of place. Ponca City was near, and she could visit the town if she wanted a change; however, she seldom did. The tenth governor of Oklahoma built Marland Mansion and there was always traffic in and out, sometimes coming to conduct state business and other times to check on oil development.

In the year-age of birds, Raven had lived a long time. It took more to excite her than most birds, but for some reason, the sound of the hounds howling and men on horseback crashing through underbrush caught her attention. A fox hunt was a regular tradition at the Mansion get-togethers, and today the spring sunshine softened the last of winter's breeze. She watched the activity with interest.

The hunters were bearing down. It would only be minutes until the little red fox was boxed in. Not that she was an unkind bird, but Raven did enjoy watching a fox get caught in a bit of a spot. Dust flew, dogs howled, and men shouted. Raven flew closer. Perched on the bonnet of her favorite sculpture, a pioneer mother and child, the curious bird leaned into the direction of the commotion waiting to hear the hunting horn sound in victory, announcing that the fox was caught.

In a surprise turn of events, the red, furry animal escaped. "Caw-ha." Raven was a tidbit disappointed, but she was also an optimist. No doubt, the afternoon hunt would be successful. Raven knew Mr. Marland liked letting the dogs loose to enjoy the chase. Even some of the window guards for the mansion were designed with the likeness of dogs sculpted on the metal bars.

The estate grounds were decorated with sculptures everywhere. Raven often combed her feathers perched on one of them before flying across the lakes circling the castle like a moat. She liked seeing her reflection in the water. On cloudy days, the broken bit of mirror that adorned her nest would show if a feather was out of place.

Raven liked looking good. While waiting for the afternoon show, she found a sun-warmed window ledge and began to pick and preen her feathers until they shone. Each black spear reflected quite like a mirror, and Raven puffed her chest in pride.

The open window let the fresh air fly past her into the cavernous room at her back. All was well, until she spied a red spot on her left wing. "How can that be?" Raven pecked at the blemish. No matter how hard and fast she pecked, the red remained. "I'm ruined," she wailed and was about to pull out the offending feather when the spot moved.

"Squawk?" Raven whirled around. In front of the ballroom fireplace shivered a small frightened fox. "You," she sputtered in anger, "your red fur is messing up my shine."

Fox's nervous movements set his tail shaking. Brought to Oklahoma, on what he thought would be a very fine vacation, Fox apparently didn't plan to lose his fur racing to escape hounds, or listen to idle chit-chat debating its merits. He ignored Raven and instead focused on the two snarling dogs he faced.

Chapter Two

"Caw-ho, Fox! Get out of that castle. What are you doing in there anyway?"

"Quiet, you obnoxious blackbird," Red Fox panted. "My life is at stake. Didn't you hear the thundering horse hooves and the shouts from the hunters? They made the earth shake and my knees quiver so that I could hardly run anymore. I crawled through a door crack into this cave. But now, I am afraid of these dogs."

"Caw-haw," Raven chirped. Fox had called her a blackbird when everyone knew she was a raven. "You are not in a cave, you silly, trophy fox. You are in the great Marland Mansion, the Palace on the Prairie." Raven announced with pride.

"Those dogs in the fireplace aren't even real," she taunted through the open window. "Maid Mercy calls them 'dirty andirons'. She doesn't like cleaning them. They are harmless. They never move, even when hot fire burns at their tails while consuming the log they carry on their backs. See!" Raven flew through the window and landed bravely on one of the dog's heads.

Raven thought Fox was quite dimwitted. "You might as well crawl up on the mantle and join the trophy lineup," she cawed.

Red Fox's fur bristled. He looked from the dog-faced metal supports holding a log in the fireplace up toward the mantle. The row of gold and silver fox-topped trophies looked like relatives. He gulped.

"Yes, indeed," said a very smug bird. "I bet the master will want your likeness on a trophy up there, too."

Only a smidgen of a quiver was apparent in Fox's voice. He bravely replied, "You can't scare me for I am already so scared I cannot spare you any feeling."

Raven cackled. "Can't scare you, huh? Well, how about this? You are hiding in a castle that belongs to the chief hunter around here. I think I hear him gathering more hunters."

Red Fox groaned. "Oh, if only I had stayed in Pennsylvania. My cousin told me that getting caught was folly. But no, I didn't listen. I wanted to see the world. Oklahoma sounded like such a nice place to visit. Now look at me. I'm here, and trouble waits for me around the corner."

Raven couldn't help herself. Call her a blackbird, would he? "And the Mistress of the Palace, why Mrs. Lydie is probably in her bedroom sipping tea and toasting your demise. For if you are not caught, her party will not have a trophy to set on the main table tonight. You are a stewed goose so to speak..." Raven prattled on, "a fox in a box of trouble."

"Hush your chatting. My mother warned me not to pay attention to birds like you."

Hmmm, his mother warned him of me, Raven thought. She puffed her chest. "I have always known I was a bird of worth." She was so caught up in herself, Raven didn't notice an old enemy advancing.

But...Red Fox did. "Watch out!" He cried and tucked into a furry red ball to hide behind the once feared dog andirons. From the sooty crevice of the fireplace, he spelled out a warning, "C...A...T."

Whoosh! Intent on snatching a piece of fresh bird roast, the furry Castle Cat of First Degree bounced from the door of the ballroom toward Raven who was trying to figure out what C-A-T spelled.

11

"Ca'at," she sounded out and her feathers fluttered in alarm. She blasted off toward the direction of the window.

All muscle beneath his furry coat, Sarge gave chase. Unfortunately, instead of bird belly, the long sharp spikes of the castle cat's claws only furrowed the window sill stone as he dug in trying to save himself. Hanging from one claw, the cat pulled back onto the ledge, safe.

From a leafy tree, Raven gave a weak but triumphant, "Caw-ho." The fouled feline flattened out to wait.

Victorious scars from other battles lined up on the cat's shoulder like stripes on a soldier's uniform. He wore them proudly and took his job very seriously. His green eyes stayed glued to the tree. He would show that bird who was boss at the Marland Mansion.

Raven thought about telling the cat to look for the tasty red tidbit of fox behind him, but she couldn't, especially since Fox's warning had saved her from the belly of that pesky feline, Mr. Sarge. Raven settled down to quietly wait for the cat to sniff out a rat in some other part of the castle.

Sarge didn't give up easily and licked his fur first one way and then another, always keeping an eye toward Raven. "Raw, I like bird raw," he taunted.

Raven hopped from one wobbly foot to another, peering anxiously from behind the leaves. Not until the hunting horn announced the afternoon hunt did Sarge grow bored with watching the bird prance in the distance and give up. His grumbling stomach would have to settle for mouse kabobs.

Red Fox heard the huntsman's horn and moved further into the black cavern.

The tiny movement caught Sarge's eye. He jumped from the sill to the checkerboard floor. "What's this?" Sarge clawed at the rings hung on the necks of the dog andirons. "Do I spy a bit of trembling fur?"

Fox cringed and tried to hide better. Soot from the fireplace rained down when his tail brushed against the brick.

The cat drew closer and closer to the frightened fox, when suddenly, Raven's caw-haw caused him to twirl around. His bristled neck hair pointed first at Raven, then back toward the fox. Lunch, would it be bird or fox? The famished Mr. Sarge, the Chief Castle Cat, Rodent Guard of First Degree, arched his back and snarled his most menacing meow and tried to decide...maybe both.

Raven looked for all the world as if she had nothing to fear. Smiling, if a beak could be said to smile, she nonchalantly snubbed Sarge.

Sarge bristled from the insult. "I'll show you who's boss around here," he hissed. Like an exploding star, the spiked fluff of indignation sprang at the feathered fowl.

"Caw-haw." Raven flew out the window. The miffed cat clawed air right behind her.

Seeing Sarge sprawled flat tickled Raven clear to her wishbone.

Poor Sarge. Dust flew like embers from a campfire on a windy day. He shook his limp body. With what dignity he could muster, and one less of his nine lives, the cat hobbled across the grassy plain, mumbling and promising retaliation...later, when he felt better.

Raven caw-hawed once more before turning to check on Fox. "Are you still there?"

"Barely," came a weak reply.

"Well, come on out, you're safe now."

Red Fox shook off the black fireplace ash. "Would you fly me out of the castle to a safe place in the woods?"

"I can understand why you believe I can do anything," Raven crowed. "But little as you are, foxes are a mite too heavy for transport by friendly Raven Air."

"What am I to do?"

"I've been thinking. I have not only saved your life, but I think I have a way to help you out of your dilemma...that is...if...caw-ahem, you will help me confiscate a particularly large jewel I've had my eye on."

"Confiscate? You mean steal?"

"Steal is such a harsh word. I just want to move it to my abode. My nest will be so elegant, and the jewel will be safe there."

"Can a raven bird ever be trusted?" Fox asked.

"Think about it. The jewel is too heavy for me to fly it out the window. I might drop it and lose it. But, if I rode on your back and showed you the way out of the castle, I wouldn't lose the jewel, now would I?"

"Hmmm. Why does that sound perfectly logical?"

Chapter Three

Encouraged, Raven went on. "Now, I know foxes and ravens are not especially favorable toward each other, but I'm willing to make an exception. I know every opening in the castle, including the small hole in the furthermost corner of the kitchen, beneath the brooms and dust mops."

"Well, you do seem quite confident."

"Of course I am, and it's a better idea than the mistress turning you into fox stew and wearing the jewel around her neck at dinner. If you help me..." Raven reasoned further, "you will be free. I will have the jewel, and Mistress Lydie will wear her second-best necklace and serve cabbage soup, which is not as tasty as fox stew, but—"

"Okay, okay! I'll help you." Fox swallowed his fear and took one cautious step forward, then another. His fur caught on something, and he imagined a gruff growl. In Fox's frenzied eye, it wasn't fur caught on an andiron that caused the tug, but the steel jaws of a metal dog set to chew him to bits.

Red Fox had a vivid imagination. "Yipes!" he cried. Thinking he heard snapping and snarling, the little fellow slipped out from the fireplace and slid down one row of checkered floor and up another.

Raven fluttered above. "Stop, Fox. Stop!"

"I can't. Dogs are trying to eat me."

"Dogs, shmogs." Raven caw-hawed at the funny idea of the big metal andirons coming to life. "I told you those dogs are not alive."

Fox, rather sheepishly, flounced his bushy tail at the now quiet dogs and followed after Raven.

"Shhh, Mistress Marland's room is close."

"Where?" Red Fox panted. Tall walls and deep spaces loomed everywhere. Dancing dark shadows drifted back and forth playing a game of chase with weakening sunbeams. Candles flickered from the wall sconces.

"Snap, crackle, fizz."

"Did you hear that?" Red Fox scrambled closer to Raven.

"What?"

Fox twitched his ears and looked carefully around. "Oh, nothing...I guess."

"Pop, fizz..." And, the sound of the small flame at the end of the candle wick seemed to say, "I smell fox hiding in my foyer."

Had Fox known that the Fire Man was just an iron wall decoration cradling a spattering, sputtering candle he might not have ran. Caught and hung on the wall as securely as Lady Laundress pinned socks to the clothesline in the yard, the talking candle flame was harmless. Fox made a mad-dash race from an enemy he couldn't even see, but only imagined, in order to outrace fear.

"Now what?" Raven croaked.

Fox and Raven were lost in a maze of black and white checkered floor tiles when they both ran out of steam. That was also when they heard the footsteps.

Thump, thump, thump, the sound was coming nearer.

17

Fox was too tired to move. For once his imagination was quiet.

But, Raven knew. Footsteps meant people. People meant danger. She clutched onto the fur at Fox's neck. Up. Down. Up. The load was too heavy for her to carry away. Up once more and the fur slipped from Raven's grasp. As luck would have it, or not, Fox fell on the Fire Man candle holder fastened to the wall.

Raven ordered, "Stay there," and she promptly disappeared.

"Snap, crackle, pop...flames will soon toast fox fur," Fire Man seemed to taunt.

Caught in Fire Man's grip, Fox did what any frightened fox would do...he fainted. He hung as limply as a fur collar on a fancy coat rack, not caring at all that Fire Man continued to spit and fizz.

Thump, thump, thump. Master Marland walked down the hall. He was going to tell Cook that the afternoon hunt was not successful, no fox, not even a blackbird to bake in a pie. Passing beneath the candle sconce, the master grabbed the fur hanging there. "Hmmm," he pondered. "I wonder why my wife left her coat collar on the candle holder. Didn't she know it might get burned?" He tossed Fox over his shoulder.

Raven watched the whole drastic scene from a high corner.

"Cook," called the master. "Gather the cabbage and brown some toast. We'll not have fox stew tonight."

Cook looked blankly at Master Marland. *Wasn't that a fox around his neck?* "No fox stew?" he asked.

"None," the master answered. "Oh well, I would have turned the fox loose if we'd caught one, so that we could hunt another day." He smiled before turning to leave.

The cook shrugged his heavy shoulders and went back to punching the bread dough. No matter whether cabbage or fox stew, he must still make bread.

Raven followed Master Marland, staying in the shadows. She perched on Fire Man and watched and waited, delighted to see Master Marland disappear in his wife's room and come back out minus Fox.

In her excitement at the good fortune of getting Fox into the mistress' room with the help of Master Marland, Raven lifted off in flight with a rush of wings. No doubt this good luck meant she was to have the gem after all.

Raven's quick movement caught Fire Man's flame. A small sizzle, sputter and the candlelight went out. Raven never noticed.

She was finally to have her treasure. "Fox, Fox! Wake up." Raven chirped. Nothing. The fox did not move. The frustrated bird flew to the jewelry box, stuffed and running over with bright baubles and trinkets of every color in the rainbow.

21

Chapter Four

Normally, Raven would have picked up a small jewel to match the others she had already stashed about her nest. But, ever since she had seen the beautiful red stone in the shape of a heart, she had pined for it. She really wanted the jewel. She raced back to Fox and cawed until she was faint herself. Raven sighed. How could she wake Fox?

Swish, swash. Maid Mercy was mopping the hall.

"Aha-caw." Raven croaked and cocked her head. The sound of wash water was very near. She flew out to check. Sure enough, Maid Mercy was definitely busy with her mop. An apple-dumpling type of girl, Maid Mercy's cheeks fairly shone with rosy good health. Into the water and out again, the stone floor shone bright and slick.

Maid Mercy danced along. With each push of her foot, the bucket of water sailed closer to Raven. It was now or never. Into the suds the bird dove. Dripping water from beak to toes, she flew in and shook her wet feathers over Fox's head.

Red Fox gasped.

Raven twisted and turned until she had no more water to shake out.

Finally, Red Fox woke. "What happened?" he asked.

"You almost cost me the chance to get my jewel, that's what. Hurry, get up. Maid Mercy is headed this way. We must get my ruby and be gone before she arrives."

Red Fox barely had time to say okay before Raven had pushed him over by the dresser right below the treasure box of jewelry. "Stay right there. I'll get the jewel and drop down on top of you. When you feel my weight, run." Raven ordered.

Poor, tired Fox gave a small nod.

Raven picked and rearranged until she moved the red, red ruby to the right spot. At last, she grabbed it in her beak, and then…vanity, oh vanity, Raven looked into the dresser mirror. *Oh my,* she thought, *the red of the jewel is so bright and such a striking contrast to my beautiful black plumage.* Raven turned and with each turn, pride crept further into her heart. "How very beautiful I am," she cawed.

Maid Mercy's swish-swash came closer. Raven could not resist a final look. She puffed out her chest to the limit and off rolled the ruby…dropping right onto Red Fox's furry back.

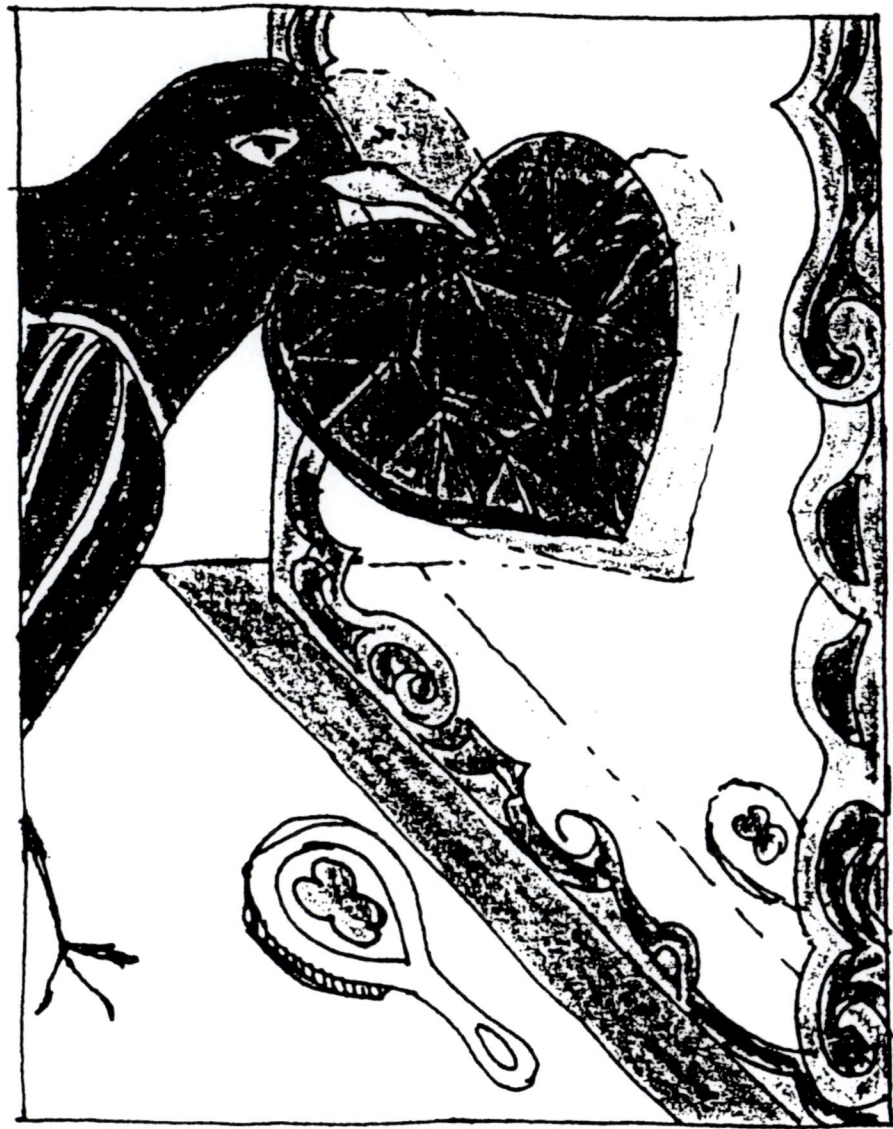

Fox felt the weight and did just as Raven had ordered, he took off. The ruby jostled joyfully along, resting in a nest of soft red fur. Fox was at the door when a rather large foot pushed a pail of water right in his path. He hit the bucket hard. Water sloshed everywhere, and the jewel went flying.

Horrified, Raven dove quickly and caught the jewel in mid-air, and a bit of soapy water hit at the same time. The ruby slipped out of her beak and into a fluffy fold in Maid Mercy's red and white striped skirt. It shot like a bullet down the muslin slide right into the sloshing bucket of mop water.
   Fox laid groggily over to one side. A frustrated Raven zoomed down and pecked his nose. That brought Red Fox right to life. He jumped up and got caught in a circle of darkness beneath Maid Mercy's skirt. Round and round he ran.

   "Oh, my...tee-hee. Oh, that tickles," the maid laughed. She danced about only making things worse. Fox moved fast to keep from being stepped on. The more his fur tickled Maid Mercy's slippered feet, the more she protested.
   "Oh, stop...tee-hee!" Maid Mercy bent over double with laughter. She couldn't stop jumping, and Fox couldn't stop running. Finally, she laughed so hard, she fell to the floor and rolled over and over and over.
   At last, Fox could see. Free from the buffeting hemline, he faced a furious, blackbird.

"Now look what you have done."

"Me? What are you talking about?"

"My ruby is in Maid Mercy's scrub bucket." Raven gave a disgusted chirp.

Maid Mercy still rolled round and round in her petticoats and striped skirt. Her apron was over her head, and her mob cap that had once covered her hair was now on her foot.

"What's wrong with her?" Fox asked, panting between words.

"Never mind. Come on. We've got to get out of sight until I can figure out a way to get that jewel back."

"Jewel, shmewel," Fox huffed. "There's a time to stop running."

"Okay," said Raven. "I warned you. When Maid Mercy gets on her feet, she's going to grab you by the neck and take you straight to Cook."

"I'm not scared." Red Fox stuck his nose straight up into the air and ignored Raven's fluttering. He was so busy *not* being scared that he didn't notice Maid Mercy until the red-cheeked lass looked straight into Fox's green eyes from only a nose length away.

"So, you are the little culprit that tickled my feet. Cook will be glad to see you."

That simple statement hung in the air. Fox didn't move until a dimpled hand grabbed him by the fur of his neck. "Come along, my little playful pet. I have work to do, and Cook's stew is waiting for fox flavoring."

Raven's heart thumped. "Oh me, for vanities sake I have lost my precious jewel!"

"What about me?" gasped Red Fox.

"Let me think. Let me think." Raven repeated from her high perch.

Maid Mercy straightened the hair beneath her cap and patted the apron straight with her empty hand. Cook would surely be impressed with her find. Tucking Fox securely under one arm, the maid used both hands to tie her slipper.

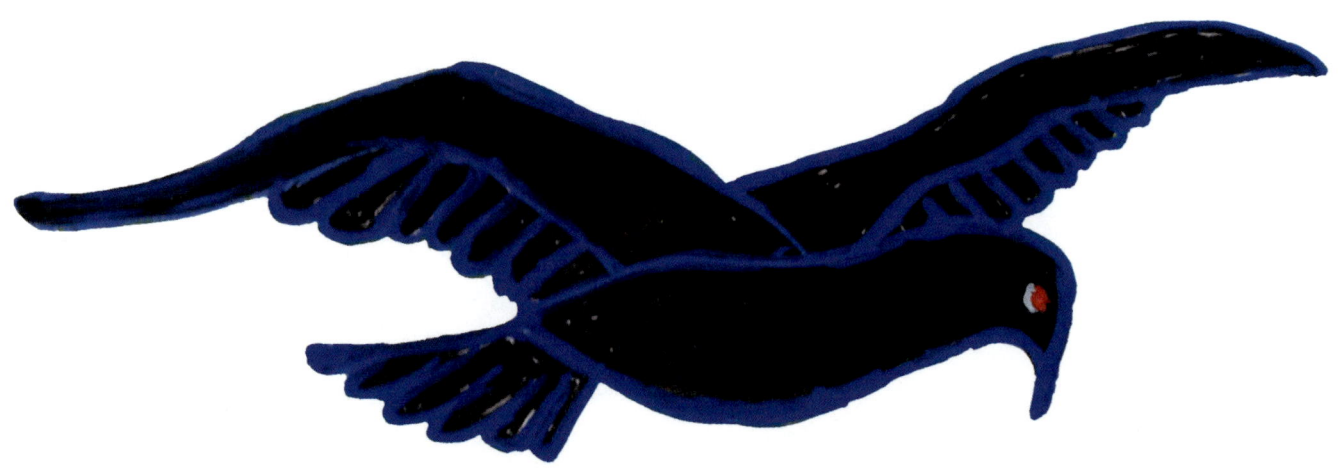

With a steep dive, Raven did the only thing she knew would make the caught fox jump. She pinched his nose hard with her beak.

"Ouch!" Red Fox wiggled out from under Maid Mercy's arm and landed right dab in the bucket of soapy mop water. He came up gagging. The bucket tipped on its side. Fox, water, and ruby raced toward the startled maid. "Help!" she cried before being carried away in the swell.

A *bump* and several *ka-thumps* later, all three landed in a heap, Maid Mercy beneath and Fox perched on her head, where a dainty cap once sat. The jewel was caught right on the edge of the apron pocket, not quite in and not quite out.

All the commotion brought the big, burly cook running. *Ka-thump, ka-thump, ka-thump.* Seeing his favorite maid tumbled in a pile at the foot of the steps, he cried out, "Mamma mia! What has happened, my little maid? Are you hurt?"

At the great cook's concern, Maid Mercy blushed until her red face blended with Fox's red fur. Finally, she sputtered. "The fox, Cook, I brought you the fox."

"Oh, my little cupcake, my bloom in winter, who cares for the fox? It is you I love."

Maid Mercy all but swooned at such grand attention. The cook was a very strong and handsome man.

To emphasize his feelings, Cook flung the fox toward the door. Raven watched with bated breath, her eyes focused on the red, red ruby. If only she hadn't looked in that mirror.

"Here, my sweet potato," Cook crooned. He held his arm out toward Maid Mercy and picked up a corner of her apron in his other hand. "Let me dab the soap suds from your nose."

Raven gave up. Shoulders slumped in defeat, she flew toward the open door. But, before she was past the threshold, Cook touched the apron to the maid's pert little nose. "Hooray!" From the apron's wavy depths, a very bright, red treasure tumbled out.

It tumbled and turned and spun to a stop. Raven was not one to look a gift horse in the mouth, so she picked the jewel up and jumped square on Fox's back. They raced past sculptures, both big and small, men of stone and dogs of metal, lions of marble and fountains of foaming blue water. Gargoyles hung from the roof eaves and watched them pass.

Chapter Five

Where the sidewalk split, in front of a big rock, Raven balanced on one foot so she could point. Fox caught the meaning and turned right. Raven soon wished she had pointed left.

    As it happened, the chosen path passed by the favorite hiding-hole of a very plump rat. And waiting patiently at that very spot sat a very patient scout of a cat. The Rodent Guard of First Degree, who waited for the rat, was the very mad feline named Sarge.
    Sarge's ears perked up as soon as he heard fox feet padding down the sidewalk. With a snicker and a sneer, the big cat hid from view just as around the corner came the jewel-carrying crew.

"Did you hear anything?" Fox asked.

"No!" snapped Raven before she even thought. And, out from her mouth dropped the jewel like a rock.

"Awk." Raven choked. "Now look what you've done."

Raven scrambled for the jewel.

Sarge scrambled for Raven.

Fox plopped down to rest.

The jewel just happened to fall beneath Fox's paw so neat that not a bit of it showed anywhere.

No one saw the smug little fox give a smile and a nod. Back, the wise one scooted away from cat fur and bird feathers flying.

And then...came Lydie Marland. She walked daily in the woods by the way.

Fox cringed when her soft white hand and arm wound round his red, red fur. So tightly she held on, Fox knew that jewel or not, he was well and truly caught.

"Oh my," the mistress gasped when before her eyes Sarge spit out feathers and grabbed Raven by the neck. "Sarge! Stop this foray." She stomped her tiny foot, "Stop, I say."

Oh drat, Sarge thought. But being the good Castle Cat that he was, he gave a spit, or two, then calmly and very politely sat. He thought to purr his way back into Mistress Lydie's heart and onto her lap.

The queen did indeed bend to pet her scraggly cat, but Red Fox squirmed and wiggled so that finally, Mistress Marland let Sarge go.

The cat grumbled and growled at the little fox until his mistress bid him, "Go, Sarge, go."

The disgruntled feline bowed deep and ambled off, his only consolation was a feather here, a feather there, Raven's fine feathers were scattered everywhere. Sarge's whiskers shook as a smile crept up. The rat was gone, the fox in arm, but that old blackbird was taken down. "Meow," he said.

From near the rock, Raven sadly cawed and covered her bony breast as best she could. Without her pretty feathers, she didn't feel dressed. She picked here, and there, but barely did she find a hair.

Mistress Marland shook her head. "Oh, you poor bird. What has Sarge done?"

She bent to rescue the barren bird. A picture of fox stew and blackbird pie came to mind. She shook the thought right out of her pretty head and gave bird and fox a hug instead.

Raven grunted, then cocked her eye. Was Fox looking a little sly? Suspicion grew. "Caw-ha," said Raven, "did you hear that?"

"No!" snapped Red Fox before he thought. And, out from his mouth dropped the jewel like a rock.

Raven choked back a shriek.

Fox smiled sheepishly, caught like a thief.

"What's this?" Mistress asked and leaned to see a very, very red treasure. "My jewel," she gasped, and both Raven's and Red Fox's heart tightened in fear. Stew and pie, they thought were sure.

"Oh dear, my jewel was lost, but found by you two here. I and Master Marland will surely reward both of you tonight." She smiled down at the two she held and casually walked toward the castle cook.

"She did it!" Red Fox was quick to shout.

"He did it!" Raven squawked.

"Oh, how sweet you both are to give each other the credit." With a wink and a nod, she gave them over to Cook and begged the large man bend to hear so she could whisper something right in his ear.

No matter how they tried, neither Raven nor Fox heard a word she spoke.

They thought she might have said, fox stew and bird pie. "Good-bye," they sobbed, "good-bye." And off with Cook they went.

35

Dusk crept over the prairie, and guests arrived two by two, ladies and gentlemen dressed in their finery. And who do you suppose on the table sat? Right in the center, Red Fox napped. Raven was smarter than that. She preened for the guests on a mirrored plate with a red, red ruby stuck proudly on her bare, bony breast.

It was said in town the very next day, the Mistress Marland was so smitten with the two, that she quite lost her head. Instead of confining the thieves, she took them to raise and asked them sweetly to reform, faithfully promising they would come to no harm as long as they joined ranks with Sarge in the Royal Guard. And of course, they agreed.

Cabbage soup and Cook's bread were deemed the very best. At least that is what Maid Mercy told Cook when she kissed his blushing cheek until it matched her rosy red.

The only scowl seen that night was the menacing look of a very, very patient Castle Cat, Rodent Guard of First Degree.

37

SPECIAL THANKS

Mary Lou and Jerald Mowery have graciously provided funding for the publication of this work in recognition of Beverly Brewer's contributions to the Franklin County Historical Association.

THE MARLAND MANSION

The Marland Mansion was, and still is, a prairie castle of secret whispers, gargoyles and stone carvings. The builder was Ernest Whitworth Marland, oil magnate, philanthropist and tenth governor of Oklahoma. The Palace on the Prairie boasted 55 rooms and along with landscaping expenditures, cost 2½ million dollars to build. The three-story structure was modeled after the Davanzati Palace in Florence, Italy, and completed in 1928.

One of the activities Mr. Marland enjoyed most was a jolly fox hunt reminiscent of Europe's colorful tracking of fox using trained foxhounds. A small red fox, let loose on the Marland estate grounds, provided friends and visitors on horseback an opportunity to see if they and the hounds could outwit the wily animal. After the fox was brought to bay by the hounds, it was re-captured, then used in future hunts or given to a zoo.

This children's story is fictional, but contains many truths connected to the Marland Mansion. The author's hope is that children everywhere will enjoy this imagined piece and come to respect the extensive history and vision of a man who brought a little bit of Europe to the Oklahoma plains, both in architecture and tradition.

Although the grounds are no longer as they once were, Marland Mansion is open to the public and part of Oklahoma's proud heritage. Readers are encouraged to research the estate at www.marlandmansion.com or tour the Marland Mansion Museum and grounds in person at 901 Monument Road in Ponca City, Oklahoma.

ILLUSTRATOR

ILLUSTRATOR - Beverly (Boterf) Brewer lived in Ponca City, Oklahoma from 1940 until her marriage to Cletus Brewer in 1957. Her father was a chemist at Great Lakes Pipeline Company in Ponca City. The couple were educators and had two sons. Following retirement, they moved to Cypress Springs near Mt. Vernon, Texas and became active volunteers. Beverly was an exceptional, accurate artist and instrumental in illustrating a number of Franklin County Historical Association publications. The Texas award-winning Dupree Park Nature Trail Guide continues to enlighten trail users with her pen and ink drawings of plants, insects, and animals. The illustrations Beverly completed for *The Fox, the Raven, and the Castle Cat* are colorful reminders of her childhood at Ponca City and the Marland Mansion. In honor of her love for history and Beverly's many contributions to the Franklin County Historical Association, this children's book is published posthumously to inspire following generations.

AUTHOR

 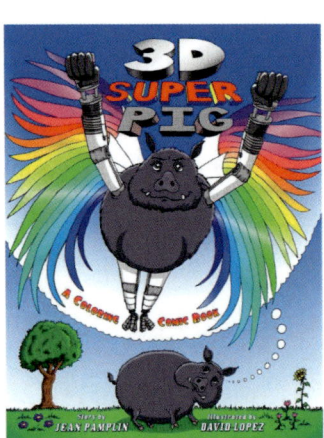 

AUTHOR - Jean Pamplin lives in Hagansport, Texas and has written, researched, and helped publish regional works for the Franklin County Historical Association, including a book about Don Meredith's hometown life before he became a famed Dallas Cowboy football player. She is published in fiction and non-fiction. Her most recent work, *3D Super Pig*, with David Lopez, is a coloring-comic book, available on Amazon. She and her husband Ed have four children and two grandchildren. Her community work includes the organization of the Northeast Texas Writers Organization (NETWO) and the Franklin County Arts Alliance (FCAA).

Made in the USA
Columbia, SC
28 February 2020